# CONTENTS

# PART 1

# BEFORE WE BEGIN

# Ya need to be able to þin this down

so ya can see it in ya mind as it plays out –
picture where it's happenin.

Imagine it's summer.
A hot one.

Leave the suburban semis to their leaf-dreams
and head for the city,
straight into the streets that surround the centre.

See how things are different?

It's tighter 'ere.
Can ya feel it?

See the take-aways and neon-washed litter?
The disfigured pigeons
huddled under railway bridges and flyovers?
Taxis    buses    pizza-boxes    vape shops?

This is not a place of labradors and lattes
and electric Audis
this is a place of staffies and cider
and exhaust-pipe smoke,

a place of one foot in front of the other brother
cos what else ya gonna do?

See that tall, skinny kid with the ball in his hand
sayin, *see ya later* to his mate?
That's me:
Nathan Wilder
Nate.

10 years old
and a week away from the end of Year 5.

# One more thing

The woman over there pushin the buggy,
hair scraped up in a top-knot,
headin to the shop for milk and cider,

a little kid
dressed as Spiderman
trailin behind her,

that's Mum.

The kid is Dylan
my nearly-four-year-old-nuisance-of-a-littlest
brother.
Always up to no good,
straight out any open door.


The bigger kid further back,
kickin stones along the road, ignorin Mum's shouts
to *GET A MOVE ON*,

that's Jaxon          or Jax as everyone calls him:
my other brother

8 years old

he's alright.

# Nearly forgot

The school ya can see       right next to the park

in the middle of the estate,

the one with the fancy new claddin
the council are puttin on top of all the
crumblin bricks and callin it
'regeneration',

the one with the main road right next to it
rattlin the claddin back off
and the corner shop opposite the main gates
where Mum's headin to,

that's Poppy Field Primary.

My school.

# These are my streets

these are my people

this is my story.

# PART 2

# SOME STUFF YA NEED TO KNOW: THE FAMILY

# Me (gonna do mine in rhyme)

Tall     thin
like to win

on-point hair
long-distance stare

love football  laughs
not down with maths

read everythin
make words sing

write            don't fight
not a coward though   right?

(Just swear I'm scared I'll lose control
of The Beast that sleeps within my soul.)

# Mum

is bonkers

says it herself
not in a 'needs lockin up' kind of way
though she has been before

she's just                    damaged
I s'pose.

Ran away at 15
been runnin ever since,
won't ever say why
or what happened to make her leave,
but it was summat           bad.

Had me at 17.

Always tryna fix someone,
people at the door with a broken wing.

Loadsa lipstick

goes to Bingo round the corner
most days
laughs a lot   loud   proper head back snortin.

Cries too,
when she thinks we're asleep.

# The story of the three wheres
## No. 1: Nick — my dad

The reason I'm tall.

Mum keeps a picture of 'em together
dun't know I know it's in her top drawer.

Looked like Jesus
she says
and I see what she means
long black hair
little beard
graceful.

He was young
too young
like Mum.

Was gonna save her
help her escape the past
right up to the point she got pregnant with me.

Got cross      got scared
got gone

went walkabout in the wilderness
never came back.

Could be dead
could be out there
still walkin

depends what ya believe.

I'm past it.

Mum'd deny it
but

she's always been lookin
for Jesus

it's just that now she only sees his face
at the bottom of a bottle
or the back of a Bingo card.

# No. 2: Brandon — Jaxon's dad

Big     bald    bear

body-builder  biceps

bouncer                              bully

beer                    beer                    beer

banks    balaclavas    bullets

behind bars

bye bye baby.

# No. 3: the question mark — Dylan's dad

A lottery

many tickets sold

no winner's yet come forward
to claim the prize.

# Jaxon

Jax
my little bro
two years below me
but nearly as big already.

Cool
clever
fast
brave
funny
lucky
good lookin
mint at football
everyone loves him.

Am I jealous?

Hell, yeah!

# Dylan

my littlest bro

calls me Natey

we call him
Turbo Terror

always movin
always sweatin
even in his sleep

thinks he's 'Spideyman'.

I feel sorry for Jax
havin to share a room with him.

Red cheeks
red hair
(big clue for the ticket-holder there)

makes Mum turn the air
blue

joinin the crew at Poppy Field
in September.

Reception won't know what's hit 'em.

We still don't.

# Oh, so ya wanna know about The Beast, right?

OK     so       it first happened in Year 2
though Mum says I was always throwin tantrums
when I was proper little
but on this day summat happened to spark it
to release it
can't even remember what it was
someone nicked my pencil maybe
or a push in the line
on the way back from assembly.

All I remember                    is                    from
somewhere really deep down in me
I feel a darkness risin        but like a hot darkness
like fire and smoke all mixed together
and my fists are flames
and the next thing I know   I'm curled up in
the Sunshine Room   cryin and cold
and, man, I'm tired         so tired
and my teacher Miss Nolan's rubbin my back and
the whole room's in bits       the whole world is.

I'd been carried out the classroom with a chunk of some poor kid's ponytail in my hand.

It happened again a week later          so they got Mum in and she had to come to meetings at school to talk about     my issues  and then I had to go see this woman every week,      Miss Hough, a counsellor,          to     talk     and     draw and find a way to keep The Beast at bay.

Two years it took us.          Two years of talkin and drawin and learnin to breathe in a way that let me control that beast, rather than it controllin me.

So if ya see me startin to breathe
in a strange way right,        I in't crazy or nothin.

I'm self-regulatin,                innit.

# Missin dad sketch me and Jax do:

Me, pickin Real Madrid on Fifa:
*How's yer dad, Jax?*

Jax goes for Barcelona:
*No Idea. He's a muppet. Don't need him.*
*How's yer dad, Nate?*

Me: *No Idea. He's a muppet, Jax. Don't need him.*

Together: *We have each other, brother!*


We're hopin Dylan'll get involved
when he can talk better
and he's stopped pretendin
to cover everythin with his
'Spideywebs'.

23

# Our house

for now

is a tiny terraced
jammed in the middle of a thousand more the same.

Landlord's a muppet
never fixes nothin
always says the rent's goin up
says he's sellin

stresses Mum out.

Gutters leak
smells                    damp,

back yard full of fadin plastic toys Dylan's smashed up.

Patch of grass over the road
NO BALL GAMES sign lyin on its side
covered in ball marks
upside-down shoppin trolley next to it.

Come in
through the front door into the livin room
which doubles as my bedroom

mind the buggy and bike
big TV propped up against the wall it fell from
sofa/bed – that's my duvet and pillow
stuffed behind it.
My pile of books.

Battered old kitchen at the back.

Upstairs is Mum's room
clothes everywhere
grotty little bathroom.

The boys' room
stuff everywhere, man.

If yer lookin for peace
go somewhere else.

# Auntie San

lives next door
her house is even worse than ours.

Mum's best mate
no blood relation
but family, y'know?

Always round 'ere
at the kitchen table
or on the front step with Mum.

Heart of gold

front tooth of one
too.

Used to be a nurse
now she dun't do much
other than smoke
drink tea and cider
and talk rubbish with Mum

they call 'emselves

dole mates.

# PS

that lad I was sayin
*see ya later* to
back at the start
with the bright blue eyes
that's Parker Smith,

my best mate since I nicked his biscuit
at nursery.

He's family
too.

# PART 3
# END OF YEAR 5

# All through Year 5 they've been tellin us

that next year will be tough
that we'd better be prepared for it
that it's a steppin stone to high school
that it's time to show what we can do
that it's SATS
that it's boosters and revision
that it's a fishbowl, everyone looks at the Year 6s
that it's time to knuckle down and focus
that it's all worth it in the end
that it's THE most important year of our lives so far
    and we need to act like it
that it's all gonna change after this year, so we need
    to enjoy it while we can
that we're gonna make ourselves proud
that it's time for us to step up and become top of the
    school
that it's the final year.

# Yeah, well, maybe, but

right now all I care about
is transition mornin tomorrow,

which kids I'll be with
next year,

cos we're a two-form entry
and they like to mix it up.

But me and PS have
always been lucky.


Oh


and who
the teacher'll
be.

# Mum's out cold still

the mornin after Bingo
so I get the boys ready
like I've done a thousand times before.
Off-brand coco pops
the dregs of milk and juice,
Dylan bangin          spillin
Jax    a wordless spoon-scrapin zombie
still lookin cool though.

Add the bowls to the twisted towers
sprawled by the sink,
Give Dylan a kiss          throw Jax a wink,
Sit on Mum's bed          *yer a good un, Natey.*

I open her curtains   she blinks at the son,

*Love ya, Nate.*        *Love ya, Mum.*

# After registers

Miss Barton reads out two separate lists of names.

One'll be the new 6G with Mrs Griffin,
who's been at Poppy Field
as long as anyone can remember
and seems like she'd rather be anywhere else,

the other'll be 6J
with a new teacher
Mr Joshua.

We go quiet
as
Miss
slowly
reads
out
each
name

| | |
|---|---|
| asks | us |
| to | make |
| two | lines |
| ready | to |
| file | into |
| our | new |
| classrooms | for |
| the | mornin. |

# I only hear two names

Nate                                    Parker

the                                     end.

# He nods at me

as his line shuffles off
to their new room.

Miss is in a rush
to get rid of us,

so she can get
her new Year 5s in.

Says she dun't wanna
talk about it,

to the kids
moanin as their

best mates go
out the door.

Says it wasn't her
decision,

she's busy
we'll get used to it.

I put my head down
and follow my line.

# PS

I'll miss ya.

# Mr Joshua

waits by the door to greet us.
I can hear him sayin, *Hi,* to the kids
at the front.

*Sit where you want for this morning
but make a sensible choice.*

I'm
dead
last.

*Hi,* he says,
*I'm Mr Joshua.*
*Welcome.*

Tall      I'm guessin the same sort of age as Mum
but looks way younger
designer glasses      footballer's skin fade
neat beard
big smile      circles his thumbs as he talks.

I do my best impression of a smile

slide past him

slump in a seat     and the smoke is risin
breathe     Nate     breathe

and I can feel the heat and the darkness and
The Beast withdraw     return to the deep

and Mr Joshua's watchin me.

*You OK fella?*
*Need a minute somewhere to chill?*

I swallow it down.

*No     thanks     I'm fine.*

# The classroom

belongs to the old Year 6
stinks of 'em
and I mean **stinks.**


Their fadin name-tags are peelin off drawers

their work is all over the walls

piles of PE bags sit underneath their pegs.


They'll be back 'ere again in a couple of hours.


This place


is              not              mine.

# He closes the door

walks to the front of the room.

*Well now, let's hope it doesn't smell as bad as this*
*this time next year.*

A few kids at the front laugh

I let myself look at him
from my slump.

He's fresh
for a teacher –
crisp skinny shirt
and chinos
black Air Force One

like he's just walked
off some fashion shoot
or summat.

He catches me lookin
holds my eye

before I turn away.

# Let's introduce ourselves,

he says,

*because after this morning*
*I won't see you all again*
*until September*
*and I'd like to know something interesting*
*about you all to take away with me.*

*Something that will help me*
*to get to know you a little better.*

He starts

tells us he was born and raised round 'ere
went to school a mile or so away
lived in the same sort of house as me

moved to London to be a musician
spent years in bands tryna make it big.

Shows us a picture of him on some sweat-soaked
stage somewhere
he's holdin a guitar          eyes closed
singin into the microphone,

but the dream died a few years back
so he came home
needed a 'proper' job                 so 'ere he is.

Tells us it's his first year as a teacher
then laughs:
*but I don't think I'm supposed to tell you that!*

Tells us he can't wait to get started.

Tells us he still loves music,
words,
football.

Tells us next year will be
fun
exciting
new
fresh
challenging

that we'll find
our way

together.

# What he dun't say:

that next year will be tough
that we'd better be prepared for it
that it's a steppin stone to high school
that it's time to show what we can do
that it's SATS
that it's boosters and revision
that it's a fishbowl, everyone looks at the Year 6s
that it's time to knuckle down and focus
that it's all worth it in the end
that it's THE most important year of our lives so
    far and we need to act like it
that it's all gonna change after this year, so we need
    to enjoy it while we can
that we're gonna make ourselves proud
that it's time for us to step up and become top of
    the school
that it's the final year.

# And he seems OK

he really does.
But all I can think of is:

PS
I miss ya.

# We do our intros

I tell him about me
but keep my guard up.

Tell him I like football too
and words and books.

He nods and smiles,

*Thanks, Nate
that's great.*

I sit back down,

listen to the others,

take in the new view.

# As we're finishin up

he plays us a song,

Three Little Birds

by Bob Marley.

He's singin as we go back to our old class

*'Cause every little thing gonna be alright!*

Whatever.

# He stops me as I leave

and goes,   *Nate*   *I want you to know*
*that I'm here to help you this year,*
*I've spoken to Miss Barton and she's told me a bit*
*about everyone from her class.*
*I know things have been tough in the past*
*and I also know how well you've been doing*
*to keep things under control.*

*I saw you doing your breathing before*

*and I want you to know*
*that even though I don't know you yet*
*and you don't know me*

*I'm already proud of you.*


And this time the heat in't from The Beast,
it's from my cheeks.

*Cheers, Sir.*

# At lunch

PS says:

*Nate*
*mate*
*stop worryin.*

*Every break and lunch*
*we'll meet up, man,*
*no problem.*
*Least you've not got Griffin.*
*Man, what a dragon!*

And then he's off
leggin it to the top pitch
where the sports coach
is tryna sort
a game of dodgeball.


*Come on, Nate!*

*Let's go!*

A poem for PS (Don't be daft, course I've not shown him — it's still on the crumpled pile I keep under the sofa, well away from Jax... and especially Turbo Terror)

We'll always be bros
so tight               so close
spirallin through every day.

We banter and laugh,
hang around at yer gaff,
don't care what the world has to say.

The knocks and the scrapes
might keep others awake
cos they've never had what we've got.

Brothers in arms
soundin warnin alarms
the friendship that never can stop.

# PS's house

is the same as mine
but
different.

He's the only kid
for a start
so he's got his own room

own space

and his mum
and dad actually go out to work
and do the things parents are normally s'posed to do.

It's calm
and I can breathe.

Spend loadsa time chillin 'ere
after school

always food in the fridge
proper nice stuff
Hula Hoops and KitKats
instead of whatever's goin cheap
in the reduced section.

# After school at PS's we get Fifa goin

like we always do,

Ajax for me
Chelsea for PS.

In between goals and throw-ins
and misses and offsides
I say: *Shame you'll be with Turner and his crew
next year.*

He says: *I'll just ignore 'em, Nate.
They're muppets!
GOOOOOAAAAALLLLL!!!!! HAAAAAA!!!
Nate, man. Ya need to stop yappin
an start playin, lad!!!*

His mum gets home,
comes upstairs in her Boots uniform,
gives him a kiss which stays on his cheek
for a nano-second
before it's wiped off.

*Out the way, Mum, he's gonna score!*

*Ya stayin for tea, Nate?*

*Nah, not tonight, thanks, Mrs S.*

# Turner

is, like PS says,
a muppet.

An absolutely
massive muppet.

The youngest of 4 brothers,

all of 'em like they've been carved out
of granite
like Stonehenge or summat
but bigger.

The 3 older ones got kicked out of high school
pretty much the minute they stepped through the door
and spend most of their time on bikes or mopeds
ridin the streets doin wheelies
wearin man-bags and scowls
waitin for dates with a judge, innit.

Turner'll end up the same.

Mrs Jones was once talkin about careers
in assembly – Aspirations Week or summat –
asked what jobs we'd like to do.

Turner's hand goes up: I *wanna be a robber, Miss.*
Cue dirty looks from Mrs Jones
and all the teachers round the side
and a playtime in the Head's office
discussin Poppy Field's **values**
and the need for **aspirations.**

Until now,
me and PS have always managed to avoid
bein lumped in his class.

He's always got a crew of **yes kids** round him
the **no kids** are the ones that get smacked.

Once got scouted by a Premier League team
scored two in his first game
got sent off
gave the coaches and the ref a mouthful
got dropped.

I trod on the back of his heel one day
playin footy on the top playground
last summer.

Told me he'd
break my nose
if I did it again.

He wasn't jokin.

Turner poem I wrote in maths after he'd been mouthin off about summat at breaktime— (I was s'posed to be countin faces and vertices of useless 3d shapes, but y'know when it flows ya gotta grab it)

Turner's no learner
he'll fight and he'll burn ya
he's done things that can't be forgiven.

Turner, man, Turner
those fists gonna earn ya
a stay in triangular prison.

# When I get in

there's a text waitin on my phone
from PS:

Yo, wot woz new teacher like btw?

Seems OK. Wot bout da Dragon of Griffinroar?

Mean, man! Proper mean!

# On the last day of Year 5

we go and watch the Year 6 Leavers' Assembly.

They do a few poems about memories,
show us photos of their residential –
lifejackets and PJs,
rope-slides and stuff –
do a little play about the school and teachers,
everyone laughs.

A few kids that have been learnin the ukulele
do summat they say is a song
but really sounds more like,
God, I don't even know.

We clap
Turner boos
has to go sit by a teacher.

When it's over
we all sing the leavers' song
that gets sung every year.

It's always the signal for tears
loadsa tears
this year's no different.

Out come the tissues
the parents cry
the teachers cry
the teachin assistants cry
some muppets in Year 3 cry
Mrs Jones, the head, cries
the Year 6 teacher, who's off to be a Deputy,
cries into her droopy flowers.

Then they get presented with a book
by some old guy that does it every year
looks like he should be dead by now
a governor or summat.

I reckon he's Father Christmas too.

Then they all go off to the dinin hall
for biscuits and juice and photos

and we head back to waste the day
watchin films we've seen ten times before
eatin cheap crisps and popcorn

and me and PS sit next to each other

all day.

# PART 4

# SUMMER HOLIDAYS

# I love the smell

of six sweet weeks of freedom
stretchin out in front of me.

We never go away anywhere.

Mum says we'll go somewhere fancy like Las Vegas
when she wins big at Bingo.

Yeah, right.

So summer is:
footy
bike rides
avoidin Turner and that lot
chillin at PS's, playin Fifa
wrestlin with Jax (and beatin him at Fifa)
tryna shake the littlest bro who's always on our case.

When I need to chill
I head to the library
and wait for PS to get back from some Spanish beach
with a tan and a rude key-ring for me.

# The first two weeks of this summer

are spent in the library
under the wing of Karen who's worked there for years.

This year, PS has gone Benidorm or summat.
So I stay 'ere and read

There's no point takin books home
Dylan'd just draw in 'em
or rip out pages
when he's stroppin.

# Jax and Dylan

have to stay with Mum
*cos they're too young*
*to go cyclin round the library*
but she lets 'em play out
on the grass verge at the front
near the road
while she gabs in the kitchen
to Auntie San and knocks back cider.

Bonkers, I told ya!

Jax spends most of the time
keepin Turbo Terror
from leggin it off somewhere
like straight into the road
cos his little legs move him
at hyper-speed
ginger hair bobbin up and down
firin invisible webs.

By the time I'm home
they're sick of the sight of each other
so some days I take Dylan to the park
next to school

and let Jax play Fifa on his own for a bit.

# When he's on a swing

it's like Dylan's in a trance
or summat.
Eyes wide open
totally quiet
for the first few swings

and


then



*Higher, Natey, Higher!!!!!!! LOOOOK
NAAAAATTTTTEEEEEEYYYYY
I'M FLYYYYYYYING!*

*I can touch the
SKYYYYYYYYYYYYYYYYYYYYYYYYYY!!!!!!!!!!!!*

*I'm SPIIIIIIIIIIIIIIIIIDDDDDDEEEEYYYYYYYYY
MAAAAAAAAAAAAN!*


We always end up there for ages, man.

# I read everythin I can find

by David Almond.

Last year
Miss Jones read us
**The Boy Who Swam With Piranhas**

and there was summat about it that hooked me.

His style

like music

like poetry.

# What I read:

**Kit's Wilderness,**
**The Fire Eaters,**
**Clay.**
But my favourite is **The Colour of the Sun**

it just got me, man.

# What I think:

Brilliant, man.
This guy's a genius.

He writes about people like me,

people from my background,

and the words just flow like
summat else, y'know?

The stories take me
to sea
and sand
and big open skies,

to places I've never been.

Gets me thinkin maybe I could do the same
about this place.

This life.

# As I'm leavin the library

Karen                 smiles at me
*You like David Almond, Nate?*

*Yeah, he's mint.*

*I knew you would. He fits you, you know?*
*You ever read* **Skellig***?*
She shows me the book,
orange and gold,
angel's wings on a kid's back.

She puts her hand on the front cover –
*I just love it         you must read it.*

My phone buzzes in my pocket.

*I gotta go, Karen     but I'll read it       I will.*

# Text from Spain:

You'll never guess who's here as well??????

Go on...

Turner... and his brothers...

HA!!!!!! ENJOY!!!!

# Jax, Jax cool as ya like

spins through summer on a second-hand bike.

Needs no mum     no dad     no me
till he stiffs that jump and scuffs his knee.

Tears his trackies     style disaster
Natey's 'ere to soothe and plaster.

High five     fist bump     back in the game
knockout smile that masks all pain.

Jax, Jax cool as ya like
spins through summer on a second-hand bike.

# Sometimes, some of the local teenagers have a water-fight on the verge outside our house — and of course they all love Jax so let us join in

Me, Dyl and Jax tearin round with 'em
balloons are bombs burstin over our heads
Dylan firin webs
Jax's skin glistenin in the sun, directin the battle
and they're howlin and whoopin, the big kids,
until someone's vape gets soaked and it's all over.

And Mum and Auntie San sit in battered deckchairs
by the front step
rackin up empties
howlin with laughter
heads back,

*My boys      my boys*
*get yerselves 'ere for a hug.*


The three of us breathless    water and sweat,
*I love ya so much     don't ya ever forget.*

# I'm tellin ya, Nate,

*his brothers are lunatics*
*but he was sound*
*while we were there,*
PS says,
handin me this year's rude key-ring with a smirk
(ya don't wanna know, trust me.)
*I reckon he's turned a corner or summat.*
*He was just          I dunno*

*cool.*


I slide the keep-away-from-parent present in my
pocket,
*Yeah, right,*

and hope he can't feel
the heat of the risin Beast

breathe                    breathe                    breathe.


*Ya still comin to Dylan's party next week, P?*

*Course, man!*

# Dylan's 4th birthday party

There's a bouncy castle
on the grass verge out front
where all the little local girls
are jumpin with Jax.

An old boyfriend of Auntie San's
who she's spinnin along
is dressed in the worst Spiderman costume
I've ever seen.

But littlest bro is proper convinced,

dun't notice the blue football socks
'Spiderman's' wearin
or the fact he stinks of fags and beer,

goes totally shy and quiet
when he sees him.

And when 'Spiderman' fires
a can of silly string he's got hidden up his
Spidey sleeve,

I swear Dylan's face goes redder
than I've ever seen it before

and he screams:

*SPIDEYWEBS*

*SPIDEYWEBS*

*SPIDEYWEBS!!!!!!!!!!!!!!!*

# After Dylan blows out the candles

and Mum and Auntie San have stopped spillin cider
while they dance to proper rascal old tunes

PS gets a message
on his phone
and says,
*Nate, I gotta go man,*
*Mum needs me.*
*Top party*
*save me some cake.*

Waves at Mum and Auntie San.
High-fives Jax, who's still surrounded by girls,
ruffles Dylan's hair,

jumps on his bike,
raises one hand to wave
as he pedals away.

*Laters*, he shouts.


*Yeah, laters, P.*

# Dylan says:

*Natey, will ya read me a story tonight?*

*Pleeeeeeeaaaaaaaaaasssssssssssssssseeeeeeee
Natey!*

He's shattered,
partied out.
Mum's staggered off to Bingo
tryna win back
the bouncy castle money she borrowed
from someone
ya don't wanna break promises to.

# After readin the same story three times

Littlest Bro says:

*Natey?*

*Yes, Dylan?*

*Was it really Spideyman?*

*Course it was, Dyl.*

*Natey?*

*Yes, Dylan?*

*Love ya.*

*Love ya, Turbo Terror.*

I kiss his hot cheek
tuck him in
head downstairs
to smash Jax
at Fifa.

# Bingoin mad

If she's been at Bingo
with Auntie San
they'll both stumble
through the front door.

Mum always trips
over the bikes,
swears,
giggles.

Auntie San always goes:
*Shhhhhhhhhhhhhhhh!!!!! Ya'll wake Nate up*
*Ohhhhhhh! Hiya Nate, sorry, mate!*

Then they both come over all huggy and kissy
breathin smoky cider-breath all over me
lipstick everywhere.

To be honest
I don't mind cos they're always
dead nice.

Off they go into the kitchen
openin a bottle of summat or other.
I drift off to sleep listenin
to the same stories
about lost loves and bad luck,
missed opportunities,
near misses,

the ghost of Jesus.


*Just one more number, San*
*that was all I needed...*

# Every now and then

before Jax and Dylan are up,

Mum'll come downstairs
make us a brew,

get under my covers
and chat about stuff.


And after a while
she always, always, always,
looks right into my eyes,

moves my fringe across
and says: *Jesus, Nate*

*ya do look like him,*
*y'know?*

*I know, Mum.*

She'll look away,
not wantin me to notice
the tears in her eyes,

*I try my best, Nate*
*I really do.*

*I know, Mum.*

*Things'll be different one day, you'll see*
*I know ya do so much to help us, Nate –*
*my little general, in't ya?*

*Love ya, Mum.*

*Love ya, Nate.*
*I wish ya could've met him*
*before he…*

*Me too, Mum.*
*Me too.*

# Summat I worry about over the last few weeks of summer

Sometimes PS dun't answer his phone
when I call him,
which is summat he's never done before.

When I ask him about it
he gets proper twitchy,
says he's been at his uncle's
lookin after his little cousin.

But I can always tell
when he's lyin,
cos he can't look at me.

*Just get on with the game, Nate*
he hisses,
starin at the screen
wavin his controller at me.
*Get off my case, man!*

And in the last week


He just seems to
d i s a p    p    e    a    r.

# Text from me to PS the night before the start of Year 6

We meetin in mornin?

# Text from PS to me

Can do

# PART 5

# THE FINAL YEAR

# The first day back

I get out the house
as quick as I can,
cos Mum's actually up and about
tryna wrestle Dylan into his uniform
and he's havin none of it.

I pour some cereal out for Jax,
who's not even bothered
about startin a new school year.

Grab my bag
and bust a groove,
to see what's goin on
with PS.

# I meet him

at the end of his road
like always.

Only today
is different;

today
he's not alone.

85

# Alright, Natey lad?

Says Turner        slidin me the side eye
as PS nods at me
kinda lookin embarrassed
but also kinda
not.

*Alright, Turner?*


As we walk
they talk
about Benidorm
and the pool
and how cool the entertainment team were
how great the chocolate ice-creams were
how fast the waterslide was
and what Griffin will be like this year.

And all I can think about is when he threatened to
break my nose.

And there's no room for all of us on the pavement
so I have to walk behind.
and PS barely even looks back at me.

And I begin
to understand
that sometimes

three's a crowd.

# Three Little Birds

we ain't.

# On the playground

Loadsa kids are there already,
lookin shiny-bright
in too-big jumpers and coats,
carryin pristine lunch-packs.

Turner and PS
go up the top pitch
and start passin a ball about,
like me and PS have done
since we went into the juniors.

But I hang back
on the main playground.

Through my new classroom window,
I watch Mr Joshua
as he darts about
puttin Post-it notes on each desk.

Mrs Jones pokes her head
into the room,
says summat to him as he circles his thumbs.

He nods
and gives her a big
smile.
He catches sight of me
lookin at him,

salutes me
like a soldier or summat.

I do an
I'm-not-at-all-embarrassed-to-be-doin-this smile

and salute back.

# NAAAAATTTTTEEEEEYYYYY, look!

Dylan's tearin across the playground
ahead of Jax and Mum who's wearin pjs
and last night's 5-pint eyes.

*Look! Spideyman goes to school!!!!*

And he fires a web at me.

*Ya look smart, littlest bro! Behave yaself!!!*

But he's beyond me already,
chargin headlong towards the climbin frame,
through the web-coated crowds.

Mum kisses me on the cheek
as Mr Joshua opens the classroom door.

Mum spots him
stops dead     flicks her faded highlights
*Is that ya new teacher, Nate?*

*Yeah, that's Mr Joshua.*

He smiles and waves at Mum.

She waves back
does the smile she does
when the landlord comes lookin for rent
and she's not got it.

Turns to me and just says

*WOW!*

*Muuuuuuuuuuuuuuuuuum!*

# Year 6J

The room smells of aftershave and new books,
all the boards backed.

*Put your coats on any peg you want,*
Mr Joshua says as we filter in.
*Find your name on your desk and*
*have a go at the activity on the board.*

I'm on a table next to Caleb,
who's good at art and always pretty quiet,
lost in thought.
He's starin at the one display board
that's already filled.
I follow his eyes to the big laminated letters:
DAVID ALMOND.
And then underneath that –
a picture of the same book Karen talked about
at the library          that kid with wings

**Skellig.**

# On the whiteboard

in handwritin so neat it must have taken him ages,
Mr Joshua's put:

**Welcome to Year 6 – what a ride it's going to be!**

**Find your Morning Activity Book from the pile on
your table –
write me a sentence that sums up how you're
feeling today:**

**I'm feeling nervous and excited all at once –
like there's a firework in my belly waiting to go off!**

I write:
**I'm gutted my best mate is in the other class.**

As he's scootin round the class greetin people,
he looks over my shoulder at what I've written.

*Don't worry,* he says. *Remember…*

And then sings:
*'Cause every little thing gonna be alright!*

He points at a big banner on the back wall
that reads
*Y6J: Every Little Thing Gonna Be Alright!*

I breathe     and     breathe     and     breathe.

# When the bell goes

Mr Joshua sends us home
a table at a time
from his position at the door
which opens out
onto the playground.

As I pass him, he fist bumps me,
*Good day?*

*Not bad,* I say.

*Nice one, Nate.*

*Sir, ya like David Almond, eh?*

*Yeah, of course! He's incredible –*
*you read much of his stuff?*

*Yeah, all summer at the library.*

*Excellent, Nate.* He points at the display.
*You read* **Skellig***?*

*Not yet         but I keep hearin how mint it is.*

*Ah, just you wait, Nate. Just you wait…*
*It'll change your life.*

And I walk out
into a crowd of mums,
includin mine
(proper made up in her goin out make-up)
who all smile and do silly giggles
when Mr Joshua says, *Hello!*

Word gets around, innit.

# I catch a flash of PS's bag

as him and Turner
go out through the gates
and onto the park.

*Ya not goin with PS?*
Jax says.

*Apparently not.*

# The Beast begins to stir

but Jax can see the signs a mile off
like he can smell the smoke
feel the heat or summat
and he always has enough coolness
to dampen the flames.

*Hey bro*          *chill, man,*
*do ya breathin thing, innit.*

Puts his arm round me.

*Let's roll.*

# What the next few weeks teach me about Mr Joshua

He's got a wife
a high school English teacher
he dun't ever stop singin
only gets cross when he needs to.

And he seems to like me.

We're lookin at poems one day
and talkin about how poetry and song lyrics
kinda blend into one.

*See, the best songwriters do what poets do,* he says:
*they talk about their life, in their own voice.*

Then we watch some videos of different poets
talkin about poetry,
why they do it and all that sorta stuff
and one of 'em says,
*I write poems because I have to.*

But he's talkin in **my** voice.

# Mr Joshua asks us to write a poem about our family

And when I read mine out
he watches me really closely

and when I finish
he lets out a deep breath,

*Nate   you're just like me.*

# At the end of the day

Mr Joshua calls me over to his desk,
*Hey, Nate*
*I just wanted to say*
*that poem you wrote was beautiful*
*there was something about it that just grabbed me*
*made me feel something, you know?*
*And that's what the best writing does, Nate*
*it's the feels you're looking for.*

He opens his drawer, *you got a notebook*
*or anything that you keep ideas in?*

I shake my head,
*just a pile of old paper, Sir.*

He passes me a notebook
a proper posh little
hardbacked black one.

*Here*   he says        *have this*
*I keep one around like I used to in the bands,*
*you've got to grab those ideas when they come*
*or else they're gone forever*
*you know?*
And he waves his hand above his head
tryna grab summat that in't there.

*No one used to tell me to write my ideas down*
*Nate   but they were just there knocking on the*
*inside of my head until I did –*
*just like the poet in the video*
*and you        I think you have the flow*
*you have to grab that pen, Nate*
*let it all go.*

He spins round in his chair
and types summat into Google,

*Now look at this*
*these are David Almond's notebooks*
*they're on display up in the North East*
*see all those mad swirls of words and pictures?*

*If you've got it in you        Nate*
*which I'm pretty certain you do*
*it's what you can do too.*

And he spins back round to look at me
proper kind look in his eyes,

*It helps you process the world,     you know?*
*All that heavy stuff we have to carry.*
Then he glances at his watch,
*Oooooops          staff meeting*
*I've got to go Nate          see you tomorrow.*

# What the next few weeks also teach me about PS

He's under Turner's spell
proper style
he's not bein mean or nothin
he's just
not there
not in the street mornin or night
not online.

The only time I see him on the playground
he's with Turner
two shadows blendin into one
he in't 'ere
he's gone.

# I start spendin lunchtimes in the school library

Explorin poetry            well
the battered few old poetry books they've got.

I like the way poets can just do
whatever they want, man,
write about anythin     anyhow,
I like the ones that write like ya can tell where
they're from, y'know?
Ya kinda get closer to 'em or summat.

Mr Joshua lets me borrow
some of his books as well
says he knows he can trust me,
*Best keep them away from Dylan though, eh Nate?*

# A poem I write in my ideas book about PS but would never EVER show anyone in the world let alone him

It's funny how ya move in the same way
kick the ball the same
the way ya tie yer laces and laugh
the way yer bag moves as ya run
all still the same.

The only thing that's different
is everything's changed.

# One mornin

Caleb's doodlin
in his activity book
as Mr Joshua talks us
through the timetable for the day,
and I'm watchin how his pen moves
and it amazes me how what's in his brain
flows down his arm so easily.

*What ya drawin, man?*
*Ah this?      This is just      stuff*
*the stuff inside my head.*

*Man, yer an artist dude*
*that stuff inside yer head is art.*
He gives a little giggle like he's proper embarrassed.


Man, the things people can do with a pen.

# You've not been chillin with PS, Nate?

Caleb says lookin up from his page,
*What's up with that?*
*He's always with Turner*
*and that load of idiots now.*

*Yeah, well times change, bro     times change.*

# The SATs talk

So when any other teacher talks to us about SATs
they go all tight-lipped
and talk about revision and hard work,
but Mr Joshua is proper chill.

It's Monday mornin after assembly
and he says he wants a SATs chat –
cue plenty of eye rolls and groanin
and he goes,
*No, no, no, not that sort of chat.*
*I want you all to understand*
*that in life*
*there are some things you just have to do,*
*and tests are one of those things.*
*However, I need you to know that these things*
*are not the be all and end all,*
*so I don't want anyone stressing out, OK?*
*All you can do is make sure*
*you're the best you can be –*
*and that's more than enough for me.*

And then he glances at the door
and goes a bit quieter
rolls those thumbs,
*I shouldn't really be telling you all this*
*because I know how important*
*some people think these tests are*

*but you know my wife works in a high school*
*and I can tell you this –*
*high schools couldn't care less*
*about what results you get in your SATs –*
*they just want you to do certain things well*
*to add up and all that stuff*
*and be able to write*
*and tie your shoe laces*
*and shower every day.*

And he says, laughin,
*You all remember how stinky this classroom was*
*when you came to meet me for the first time?*
*Exactly! So let's make sure*
*we're taking care of the personal hygiene, guys –*
*I'm not having our room known as the stinky one!*

*So*
*we do this year together, right?*
*We support each other.*
*I promise you all this,*

There's another joke groan
cos we know what's comin next…

*That's right 6J*
and he holds his invisible mic
throws his head back
and he's no longer in a classroom
in a city centre school…
He's on stage at Wembley…

*EVERY LITTLE THING GONNA BE ALRIGHT!*

# It's a Wednesday in November when the ball hits me in the back

I spin round and see Turner and PS laughin.

Wipe sticky mud off coat,
can't wipe redness from cheeks,
can't wipe hate from Turner's voice:
*Give us the ball back then, loner!*

Can't get rid of the bite in my guts
when I hear PS's sniggers.

# I'd been standin on the edge of the top pitches talkin to Caleb

about ideas
showin each other our notebooks
and watchin the kid
who's been my best mate for years sniggerin.

Jax
who's been playin on the next pitch
comes over,
*Y'alright, bro?*

# Turner goes,

*Ha, look at the state of him*
*bringin his little muppet brother over*
*to help him out.*

*What's up, Nate?*
*Ya can't stand up for yerself, dude?*
*You've always been like that though, eh?*
*You'd rather punch walls than people, eh?*
*Cos they don't whack back, innit?*

*Shut it, Turner,* Jax shouts
and boots the ball back over
to where the pair of 'em are walkin off laughin,
arms round each other's shoulders.

116

# Typical Beast, eh?

Where d'ya go when there's muppets to roast?
Always asleep when I need ya the most.

# Caleb sees the trouble on my face

*Don't worry about 'em, Nate.*
*They don't think like us...*
*I've seen the poems ya write*
*seen yer ideas...*

*Ya can do what I do*
*ya just paint pictures with yer words, bro.*

*Remember what ya said to me?*
*All that stuff goin on in yer head,*
*y'know?*

# Lunchtime ideas book poem

Don't hate, Nate,
yer better than that.
Yer a watcher,
a writer
keep The Beast 'neath the hatch.
A dreamer,
a learner
don't sweat about Turner.

Mud is just mud,
so wipe yerself clean.
And don't hate, Nate,
yer a dreamer
so dream.

# I don't notice Mr Joshua has walked into the library and is readin the poem over my shoulder

*You OK, Nate? Want to talk about it?*
*Nah, I'm OK, sir.*
*Well, listen, if you ever want to, I'm here OK?*
*I know how tricky friendships can be at this age.*
And he puts his hand on my shoulder.
*Nice poem, by the way,*
*great to see you're in the flow.*

*It's how I got started in music*
*with words.*
*I'll let you into a secret*
*I was never much good with the music*
*but the words...*

Then he pulls a book from the top shelf
and drops it in front of me,
*We start this next week in class.*
I look up at the book

**Skellig.**

# DYLANNNNNNN! COME DOWN FOR TEA!

Mum's shoutin
as I tip fish fingers and chips
onto Turbo Terror's Spiderman plate.
*Ah, Natey, go and find that lad will ya?*
*I'm already late for meetin Auntie San*
*and I'm gaspin for a pint.*

*Ah, brilliant, now I've smudged me nails.*

# Dylan comes down pale

No spidey bouncin
no webs.
*Y'OK, dude?*

No answer, just a grumpy look.

Mum ruffles his hair as she passes in a blurfume,
*He's been quiet all week,*
*his teacher phoned yesterday*
*to say he's not been himself for a bit,*
*just knackered…*
*Aren't we all, eh?* she says,
as she disappears back upstairs
to finish the pre-Bingo war-paint.

*All that school work, innit, Dyl love?*

# Text to PS

Yo dude what's happenin, man?
I thought we were tight?

Message left unread.

# We start Skellig

and straight away I'm hooked.
Every afternoon I settle in my chair
and get carried away to this other world.

The weird guy in the garage
all dusty and pale
eatin takeaways and drinkin beer

the wilderness
babies
owls.

And Mina,
man,
she's cool
a bitta mystery about that one
just her and her mum at home.

As Mr Joshua reads
he does different voices for each character
Dr Death like a proper creepy old dude.

I watch Caleb doodlin
just lines and lines arcing and flowin
across the back of some old maths worksheet
framin the spaces of his brain.
He draws wings.

We have these long chats
about what we think's gonna happen:
who the guy in the garage might be
what he's doin there
how Michael feels about movin house
bein away from his mates
and the baby.

And then one afternoon
Mr Joshua stops readin at the end of a chapter
puts the book under the visualiser
so we can see the words he's just read.

Mina's talkin to Michael about drawin
how it can make ya look at the world more closely,
help ya see things more clearly
and Caleb's watchin
and so am I

and Mr Joshua nods at me,

*Words and pictures, eh, 6J – tell your story, guys*

*tell your story.*

# We do drama sessions in the hall in pairs

It's me and Caleb.
We're all lost in the wilderness
of Michael's garden
and have to find a way out.
Then he makes us freeze-frame
and brings over one of his old mics
and starts interviewin us
all about how we'll escape,

*Any way you want, 6J,*
*be as imaginative as you can.*

People say all sorts of daft stuff
knives and rope swings,
guns and helicopters,
tanks and quad bikes.

*Nate, Caleb:*
*How are you getting out of the wilderness, boys?*

*Wings and words, sir. Wings and words.*

And most of the kids in
our class are gawpin at us
like we've got six heads or
summat

But
Mr Joshua's smilin to himself
and noddin
and almost under his breath he goes,

*Ideas, 6J.*
*Ideas guide the way.*

# At the end of the day

Me and Caleb are in the park next to school.
We talk about **Skellig** while we're on the swings.

*Yo, Nate, ya believe in angels, bro?*
*Nah, man,*
*why, d'you?*

*I dunno, not really I s'pose*
*but sometimes*
*I think there's gotta be someone or summat*
*watchin us*
*or, what's the point, man?*

# We go back to Caleb's for Pot Noodles (Bombay Bad Boy or nothin, innit?)

And man,
his house is even messier than mine
no carpets at all downstairs
white plastic garden furniture in the kitchen.

*Sorry about the state of things*
*y'know how it is*
*Dad's doin his best*
*but since Mum went he just...*
*it's like he's given up, y'know?*

*Yeah man, I get it,*
*no worries.*

# We go up to his room

And every bit of bare plaster
is covered with drawins.

It's like he's tipped out his head in there,
and right above his bed is a picture of his dad
with angel's wings.

# At school Mr Joshua goes

*Right, 6J –*
*this morning there'll be no practice papers*
*no revision or spelling tests.*

And he lines us up
and takes us out into the park by school
and just lets us play.

I mean he really just lets us play,
and stands watchin us
a big smile on his face.

# When we get back to class

Mr Joshua stands at the front and goes:
*Right, guys,*
*you know how much I've been looking forward*
*to next week's residential.*
*The Lake District*
*is one of my favourite places on Earth.*
*It's sooooooo beautiful.*

*Now your parents have all got the kit list*
*for the things you need – and remember,*
*please don't go out and start buying new clothes –*
*it's not a fashion show.*
*The place we're staying has all the waterproofs*
*and wellies and fleeces you'll need –*
*and gloves and hats...*

*I've seen the weather forecast and it's due to snow!*
*I'm sooooooo EXCITED!*
*Also, don't forget that no phones are allowed.*
*Me and Mrs Griffin will be posting a blog*
*so those of you whose parents have internet access*
*can keep up to date with all the fun we'll be having.*
*We're only there for two nights*
*so let's make sure to enjoy it.*

*Most importantly, be here on time.*
*The coach leaves at 9am on Wednesday morning...*
*Don't be late!*

He shows us a slide show of where we're goin:
a great big old house with loadsa space round it

Windermere
ropes
slides
canoes.

Man, it looks mint.

# Wednesday 8.55 am

I'm at the front of the coach next to Caleb.
Mr Joshua and Mrs Griffin on the pavement
checkin everyone in.
Kids fussin about, man,
bringin so much stuff
it's like we're goin away forever.

I got nowt much to bring anyway
so packin it into a coupla JD bags was easy.

Turner and PS and the rest of the muppets
on the back row
handin out sweets and jumpin about like idiots.

Mr Joshua gets on
*Okay guys, settle down, please.*
*Can you make sure you've got your seat belts on?*

Griffinroar comes past him
and stalks down the aisle checkin and scowlin
till even the noise boys at the back
are bound by belts.

*It's going to take about two hours to get there,*
*so just chill out and enjoy the scenery.*
*And, please... if anyone starts feeling unwell –*
*shout out and we'll get something over to you.*

He holds up a plastic bag and grins:

*I don't need any sick on these new kicks!*

Caleb turns to me and whisper-laughs:
*It's not a fashion show though, right, Mr Joshua?*

# As the coach pulls away

loadsa kids are strainin at their seat belts to wave out the window to their mums or dads or aunties or whatever.

Flailin about like babies, man.

Me and Caleb just watch 'em.

No point wavin at nobody, innit.

# We leave the city behind

and red-faced kids
burnt out from bouncin around
on their mad sugar rushes
start fallin asleep
or clutchin plastic sick bags
or just sittin like zombies.

Even the back of the coach is quiet now
as we slide out onto the motorway.

The landscape changes, man.
And all these muppets miss it.
Too busy with the rumble of tarmac
or stomach gurgles or the slow flow of sleep.

Caleb's sketchin all he can see
and so am I
in my head.

Cities blend into fields
motorbikes and scooters into sheep and cows.

The boundary line of what I know
gets left way way behind.

A black rim of distant white-tipped hills
and mountains rises in my mind
ages before I see 'em.

As we get closer

the hills are whiter than they looked:

snow everywhere

like someone's laid down feathers
on the shoulders of a new world.

# Mr Joshua's walkin back from handin out another sick bag

Stops at mine and Caleb's seats.

*See, boys... I told you! Just look at it all out there.*
*Soak it in. Food for the soul.*
*Food for the mind.*
*Feel it.*
*Draw it.*

Then he looks straight at me:

*Write it.*

# Me and Caleb get lucky

Cos we get the only room with two beds
whilst all the rest of the cattle
get lumped into rooms of 4 and 6 and 8.

# The afternoon

is spent unpackin
and then butties in the dinin room bit.
The instructors are all sound
proper red outdoorsy cheeks and hands and that

but a good laugh
the sort ya can tell proper love what they do.

The main guy, John
is barely taller than me with a little bald spot at the
back of his head and a high-pitched giggle when he
says summat daft, which is like every other word.

Dead friendly face.
He gives us a talk about all the rules and stuff.
Tells us there's machine guns in the halls
to stop boys and girls meetin in their pjs and nighties.

Says tonight we'll be doin The Night Line...

There's table football and a battered old pool table
but the you-know-who crew
take 'em both over straight away
PS avoidin eyes and Turner just starin.

So me and Caleb go scout out the rest of the place

and it's mint.

A big old house
where some posh family musta lived years ago

a massive common room
chairs all round the sides.

A dryin room fer all yer wet boots and kit
that proper kiffs like Dylan and Jax's room
if I haven't done their washin for a bit.

And the outside, man,
WOW
all fields and trees
little rivers flowin down hills

and if ya walk over to the edge
and lift yerself up onto the old stone wall
ya can see it

Windermere.

# And the words just pour out of me, man

Shifting shimmer
Windermere
veiled in rising mist.

I could live
a million years
and never tire of this.

# Snow starts fallin proper heavy as we head out for The Night Line

And I've got me joggers and jumper from home
and the Centre's wellies and hat and coat
and gloves on.

We troop out into the woods
where there's a rope tied between the trees.

John tells us what we gotta do
put a blindfold on
(I mean it's darker than I've ever seen anyway,
man, but y'know whatever)
and follow the rope
and help each other if we get stuck.

Mr Joshua and Griffinroar
are proper wrapped up too
tryna click pictures with gloves on.

I get in line in front of Caleb

and
then
it's

PS              and              Turner.

# Get on with it, Nate lad. Ya scared or summat?

I can't even see him but I can just tell
the sorta look Turner's got on his face.

Then he goes, *Can't believe we've got*
*this pair of muppets in front of us, P!*
*We gotta be smellin them trampy*
*borrowed clothes all the way round.*

Then the unmistakable sound of PS's snigger.

I feel The Beast startin to burn.

Caleb's hand on my shoulder,
*Hey, Nate, forget 'em dude*
*let's go.*

| Breathe | breathe | breathe |
| walk | walk | walk |
| follow the rope | follow the rope | follow the rope |
| stumble | stumble | stumble |
| fall | fall | fall |

*Haaaaaaaaaaaaaaaaaaaaaaaaaaaaaaa!*
*One o'them muppets just fell!!!!*
*Get past these, P, I can't be doin with 'em!*

# I'm on the ground with my blindfold round my neck

And there's a torch in my eyes.

And Mr Joshua.             And Caleb.

And hands held out to lift.

And light on snow.

# A poem I draft in my head before bed

I have fallen inside the snow

and it's OK          it's OK

to rest here a while

blanketed

because I know              tomorrow

I'll rise again.

# In the mornin, I hold a handful of snow

and watch it start to melt

and it feels kinda like it's talkin to me.

Teachin me.

What's that word Mr Joshua's always on about?

Transience.                    That's it.

Sometimes things are so beautiful
all ya can do is celebrate those fleetin moments

and accept they'll be gone.

# The lake is so beautiful

even when paddlin across it on a rickety raft
built of oil drums, planks of wood, rope
and a whole loada hope
that feels like it might fall apart any minute.

The sounds of paddles and shouts,
as we race another raft
towards the little boat in the middle
that John and Mr Joshua and Griffinroar
are wavin at us from,
disappear from my mind so quickly

that it's almost like I'm there alone.

And all around me reflects the sky
and the snow lays heavy
on the shoreline and mountains.

And, man,
I'm thinkin what David Almond
would write about this place
what flow he'd create and then

there's a sudden rumble    in the distance

and flashin low over the top of a mountain
is a jet plane, man
like a proper fighter jet
blastin round the sky
like it's havin fun or summat
and Caleb touches my arm cos he's with me too
and I'm frozen in the moment
we're frozen in the moment.

The world stops.


And it's gone.

# The other raft wins

and Turner and PS are holdin their paddles
up in the air at the front of it
like they've won the Champions League or summat

shoutin,

*Looooooossssssssssssseerrrrrrrrssssssss!*

And I swear PS is lookin right at me, man.

# Round the campfire

Mr Joshua's tryna get us to sing
some daft campfire song

but all I see is fire.

Fire and babies, man:

the only two things ya can put in front of people
and guarantee they'll be fascinated.

I'm thinkin about Dyl
how when he was a baby
and Jax was still little
I'd watch him while Mum went to the shops
for fags or whatever
and his little crop of red hair, man
sweaty as anythin as he rolled around
and I just knew I'd always be there
to watch out for him
y'know
such a tiny little thing.

And I'd stroke his cheek as he finally fell asleep.


You're safe, brother                    Natey's 'ere.


157

# The coach home

is quiet all the way

and I'm watchin
the changin sky

how darkness falls so fast.

# Now, you've never seen Christmas til you've seen it in a primary school

The whole school's like Santa's Grotto
and Mr Joshua loves it, man.

We've got little trees all over the classroom,

there's a post-box by the office
and me and Caleb get to go and deliver the cards
to each class
each day,

which means seein Turner and PS.


Well
I say seein
but they don't even look up each time we go in.
Too busy sharin jokes and chattin rubbish, innit.

# Christmas in my house

is always the same:

bacon butties
cider for Mum and Auntie San,
Dylan like a shreddin machine openin his presents
which I gotta build,
if Mum's remembered the batteries.

A coupla Nike t-shirts for me
and a tracksuit for Jax.

Then Mum gets upset,
sayin sorry    it's all she can afford.
*It'll be better next year boys*
*I promise.*

Frozen turkey:
mingin, man.

Mum and Auntie San in the kitchen
for the rest of the day
pots and pans and cans all over the place
so I always go to PS's house to find space
and pull a decent cracker.

But not this year.

# Christmas Day night

And Dylan's done.
Nappin on my bed,
paper crown stuck to his sweaty head
while me and Jax play Fifa
surrounded by Heroes wrappers.

# Midgame dad act

Me: *Yo, Jax. What did yer dad get ya for Christmas, dude?*

Jax: *Nothin, brother. What did yer dad get ya for Christmas?*

Me: *Nothin, brother.*

And then a thin voice from my way under my duvet:

Dylan:        *Hey    Natey        Jax. What did yer dads get ya for Christmas?*

Together: *Nothin, Dyl.*

Jax gives me a look.
I nod        pause the game.

Jax: *Hey, Dyl. What did yer dad get ya for Christmas?*

He sits up
looks at us both
red cheeks
red hair
red eyes
broken crown
we bump a little fist each
he smiles that cheeky smile
and goes: *Nothin, brothers. Nothin.*

Merry Christmas.

# Havin a birthday between Christmas and New Year

has always been proper rubbish, man.
Mum's a million times skinter than she normally is
and it's basically a cupcake and candle job
and:
*Nate, I'm so sorry love,*
*but you know how it is...*
*and ya did get a coupla nice t-shirts for Christmas.*

*I know, Mum, no worries.*

The only present I normally ever get is from PS

and
well
yeah
nothin
mate.


Happy Birthday, Nate.

# Yo, Nate, whassup with Dyl at the min?

Jax comes into the front room
where I've been messin about in my ideas book
after makin the tea
and tidyin up the tea
cos Mum and Auntie San
have found some proper cheap liquid tea
at a pre-Bingo New Year's Eve happy hour bar.

*Dunno, Jax.*
*What d'ya mean?*

*Well, he just seems quiet*
*and y'know he's never been quiet*
*like, when was the last time we had to tell him*
*to stop kickin a ball about*
*or stop smashin summat up and that?*
*He's spark out up there already*
*still in his Spiderman gear.*

*Yeah, man, it's startin school proper, innit?*

*He's tired*
*go wake him up,*
*help him get ready for bed, Jax*
*and*
*just*
*enjoy the chill, man.*

# I go upstairs and make sure Turbo Terror's done his teeth

Cos Jax's got the concentration span of a gnat, man
and there's no way I want my littlest bro
to be one of those kids with mingin black teeth.

*No book tonight, Natey,* he says all quiet.
*Can ya tell me a story*
*like ya used to when I was little?*
*I loved them stories.*

*Yer still little, little man!*
*But yeah, course I can.*

And I tell him about this old guy
I once dreamed about
a guy with broken wings
who only eats mice and bluebottles and takeaways

a guy who was lost
but got found.

But before I get to the end
he's gone
quiet breathin.
I watch his chest rise and fall
for a minute or two
kiss his forehead,

*Night, Turbo Terror*
*fly past the stars*
*brother.*

# The three of us

see in the New Year by watchin kids
chuckin fireworks about on the street outside.
Dyl's still proper tired
get his teeth cleaned
story
bed.


Me and Jax smashin each other on Fifa
till whatever time Mum and Auntie San
fall through the door.



A new start?
Nah, man.

# A coupla weeks into the new term

I'm walkin past the staff room
at lunchtime.

Mr Joshua comes out
still holdin half a ham butty,
*Hey, Nate, how's it going?*
*You sorted it with PS yet?*
I shrug.

*Ah, you'll get there.*
*You two go way back, yeah?*
I nod.

*Well that stuff's deep, Nate.*
*All this with Turner – it'll pass.*
*How are the ideas coming along,*
*you in the flow still?*

*Yeah, sort of, Sir*
*but all this stuff with PS*
*y'know*
*sorta stops it sometimes.*

*Yep, I know what you mean.*
*It's the chaos of life, Nate*
*the ups and downs*

*but it all feeds it, you know?*
He points at his head
butty-crumbs fallin into his fringe.
*Maybe not right now –*
*sometimes you're just a sponge*
*soaking it all up,*
*loading the pen with ink,*
*waiting for something to come along and make it*
*flow again.*
*Always does.*

*And anyway,*
*you and Caleb seem to be getting on really well?*

*He's a good kid.*
*You're a good match.*

*You'll always find your people, Nate.*

# I walk round the corner

and there's PS and Turner
messin about with a ball at the end of the corridor,
laughin and jokin.

I spin round without bein seen,

go out the other doors.

Breathe, Nate, breathe.

# Outside, Caleb's sittin on one of the benches by the field

ignorin the lunchtime organisers
who want him to get involved
with a game of tag rugby.

*What ya drawin*
*dude?*

*I dunno*
*y'know*
*just whatever comes, innit.*

I sit down next to him
open my ideas book

wait to see what comes.

# The noise

tears me out of sleep

then nothin for a second
but blackness.

Then it starts again

and at first
I'm thinkin,
it's a dog
or a fox
or summat in pain
out on the railway lines.

But when it starts again
it's louder than
an animal could ever be
and it fills the house
the kitchen
the hall
the stairs
the landin

and it's pain

and the noise is
Mum

and I'm runnin upstairs
and she's on the landin
and she's holdin Dylan
and she's screamin at him to wake up
and he's not wakin up
and his mouth is open
and his eyes are open
and his arm is floppy
and she's runnin round the house with him
holdin him
and she's screamin
and Jax is screamin
and he's not wakin up
and his eyes are open
and sirens
and doors
and ambulances
and paramedics
and beeps
and screams
and Auntie San
and they press his chest
and his eyes are open
and his mouth is open

and they stop pressin his chest
and Auntie San pulls me and Jax away
into the kitchen
and Mum's makin those noises again
she's screamin
and there's loadsa voices
and the front door closes
and sirens

and Dylan


is gone.

# A 4am simple lesson in tenses

I **had** two brothers: past
I **have** one brother: present

# I walk the playground lines

and wait for Auntie San and Jax.

Had to get out early,
walls too tight to breathe.
The caretaker checked his watch as he let me in the
    gates.
A wagtail bobs about in between puddles.
These eyes are heavy, man.

Mr Joshua's in the classroom writin the date,
spots me,
classroom door opens out onto the playground,
*Nate, are you alright?*
*You're*

*so early.*

And I'm huggin him
and now the tears come
and the words are a blur.

*Nate – I'm so sorry.*

*Sit down.*

*Nate, there are no words.*

He passes me some water
and I tell him everythin that happened last night.
He takes his glasses off,
wipes tears from his beard.

*Nate, whatever happens    I'm here.*
And that's all I need to hear.

He puts his hand on my shoulder.

*Remember*
*you have your ideas book*
*yeah?*

*And*

*Nate, I need you to know that all is not lost.*
*I want you to remember that, OK?*

*All is not lost.*

# Me and Jax

sit on the blue plastic chairs
outside the school office
where ya normally wait
to be picked up if yer poorly or in bother.

Inside Mrs Jones' office
Auntie San is talkin quickly
I can tell she's cryin
but can't make out all the words.

I hear:
*they need to be 'ere*
*I need to find her*
*she must still be there*
*her phone's off*
*I don't know*
*I don't know...*

Mrs Jones says summat I can't hear
and a chair scrapes
then it's quiet and I imagine
her huggin Auntie San.

Her office door opens
and Auntie San comes out with a tissue
*I need to get to hospital*
*to be with yer mum, boys.*

*Mrs Jones knows what's happened*
*she'll look after ya.*

*Me and Mum'll be back*
*as soon as we can,*
*I promise.*

There's a flash of gold tooth
in an attempted smile.
She kisses Jax on the head
wipes a tear from his cheek
with her tissue,

touches my shoulder.

Mrs Jones comes out the office,
pulls us both towards her.
*Come on, boys,*
*come inside.*

# In the cave in The Sunshine Room

me and Jax are sittin in silence
listenin to the normal school noises
but nothin
absolutely nothin
is normal
in 'ere.

# Mr Joshua comes in and sits down

And he dun't say anythin for a bit.
Takes his glasses off and lays 'em on the table.
Circles his thumbs
breathes really deeply
and I can see his heart beatin through his shirt.
And then he goes,
*Boys*
*Mrs Jones wants you just to chill together*
*in here this morning*
*just until Auntie San's back,*
*if that's OK?*

Jax nods.

*There'll be an adult next door*
*and people will check on you all day.*
*There's paper and felt tips and paints and things*
*if you feel like messing about with stuff.*

I see my reflection in his glasses


but I am not 'ere.

# The space

## between me and Jax

has never needed to be filled with words.
And today in the darkness of the Sunshine Room
it's no different.
And the clock ticks


and we breathe.

# Jax draws a picture of Dylan

but the orange felt tip's got no lid and won't work
so he gives him fiery red hair
and when he shows me
we laugh
so hard
we cry.

# Mrs Jones and some others

bob their heads in every few minutes to check on us
but there's nothin to say.

We don't go out to play at break,
just sit
I get my ideas book out
but the pen is empty
so I just start swirlin it round and round
and the lines get blacker and blacker
and it's smoke and darkness
and heat.

*Yo Nate*

*Please, man,*         *breathe*
*not now*             *not now.*

I count the breaths
and the spaces in between the quiet bits
and I find myself in Michael's garden
deep in the wilderness
a blackbird watches me silently
and Mina's in her tree
those eyes, man,      those eyes.

And The Beast is held back.

# Mr Joshua comes in just after break with his copy of Skellig

*I thought you might like to carry on reading,
Nate?
You know,
see where you get to?*

# I read about William Blake seein angels in his garden

about Michael's baby gettin poorly
about his mates fallin out with him
cos they miss him
about truth and dreams and how they merge into one
about wings and shoulder blades
and Chinese takeaways and aspirin and arthritis
and cod liver oil and brown ale
and dead things left by owls
about fledglin blackbirds just out the nest
so delicate      and fragile
about **Skellig**
and he's holdin Mina's hand
and he's holdin Michael's hand
and they're in a circle
and they're flyin free.

# A little while before lunch

PS comes in and sits down at the table.
He puts his head down.
His eyes are full
and he reaches out his fist to Jax
who turns away.
And now his tears come.
He reaches out to me
and I reach back
and our fists bump
and he opens his fist
and there's one of Caleb's pictures on his palm
tiny    and    delicate
and as he leaves, he slides it on the table next to Jax
who touches the outline of Spiderman with his
fingers

and follows the lines to his back to trace the wings.

# Just as the lunch bell goes

the door bangs open
and it's Auntie San
sweaty and red
fringe slicked down across her face.

*He's not dead boys he's not dead boys*
*he's alive! Boys boys, Dyl's not dead he's*
*alive boys he's not dead he's not dead*
*boys he's alive!*

She grabs us both and hugs us and I can't make out
what she's sayin at all but it's good and she's happy
and she's sad and she's tired and we hold hands
the three of us and we circle together
there in the Sunshine Room
and I close my eyes
and I swear for a second

we're flyin.

# When we land

Mr Joshua's with us
and he smiles at me.
*Auntie San told us the news on her way in, boys*
*I'm               I'm               I'm so...*


And he turns away
and sunlight catches the side of his face
turnin his tears to crystals
to whirlpools,
to dreams,


*I'm so happy for you.*

# We're sittin round the kitchen table

as Auntie San does her best
to read aloud the leaflet the doctor gave her
but gives up and looks at us both,
*He's alive boys*       *they brought him back*
*he's*   *not with it though*     *in and out of sleep.*
*They say it's called CHD*
*A Congenital Heart Defect*
*or summat like that, I dunno.*
*Too much doctor talk about infected valves and stuff.*

*It's like a tickin time bomb*

*and no one knew*
*Dylan had it*

*and no one knows why*
*it happened,*

*why the bomb went off*
*inside his chest*
*last night*

*but it did*
*and he's poorly     boys          really poorly,*
and she's cryin now and we're cryin
and she pulls us together.

*But we're fighters aren't we, eh? Aren't we?*
*Always have been     always will be.*

*Ya don't come from these streets and just give up*
*and Dyl's a fighter boys,*
and she kisses the pendant on her necklace
like she does before Bingo,
*and we fight  boys          we fight*
*and we keep the faith*
*and we've still got hope.*

# Poem for Dylan

I imagine there are tubes and wires and bleeps
I imagine your eyes are closed
I imagine the sweat on your head
and the slow red flow around your body
I imagine doctors
I imagine Mum sipping tea
red lipstick marks on a paper cup
I imagine the blackness in your head
the stars you're skipping past firing webs
I imagine your little body is tired
I imagine you on a swing
great big white wings at your back
and Dylan    my brother
I imagine you are frightened.

So                        am                    I.

# I hear the keys in the door

and Mum collapses on the sofa,
curls up under my duvet
all legs and arms and greasy hair
and tears and sweat.

I hold her
she feels so thin and small
I can feel the back of her ribs,
her shoulder blades.
My arms are round her.

*He's alive, Natey. He's alive.*

*I know, Mum. I know.*

She puts her head on my chest
and in seconds she's asleep.
She smells of hospitals
she smells of Dylan.
And it's just me and shadows now

like it always is.

# There's no cereal left so I butter some toast for me and Jax

as Mum comes in from another world,
pulls up a chair and lights a fag.

*Right, boys – 'ere's what I know,*
*I'm tryin to get my head round it all.*
*They reckon Dyl's always had summat wrong*
*with his heart, summat weird with it,*
*but it never got noticed, y'know?*
*And the bit that's not right's got an infection...*
*god knows from where, but whatever... it's there.*
*And that's what happened...*
*his heart couldn't cope... and it just... it gave up...*

She takes a big drag, wipes her eyes
and lets the smoke hang between us
swirlin like a ghost.

*Anyway, they brought him back in the ambulance...*
*I swear, boys... I thought he was...*
*And now he's on a drip.*
*They've gotta fill him with antibiotics*
*and hope he can fight....*

She stubs out the fag, her eyes are somewhere else.
She sighs. Ties her hair up in a bobble.

*Ya don't need to go in today boys*
*but          I need to get back to hospital*
*y'know,      I need to be there when he wakes up.*
*He's just driftin…*

Jax blinks back a look I've not seen before
like he's a million miles away      in the wilderness
and I think how small he looks there in his pjs
so small     then he's back      talkin,
*Nah, Mum – it's sound I'll go in,   he says,*
*might as well see my mates, innit?*
*Score some goals.*

*Me too, Mum.*

199

# On the way to school, Jax starts to talk

eyes straight ahead, unblinkin.

*Nate   ya need to know*
*I've always looked up to ya, right?*
*All that stuff ya do*
*the breakfasts*
*the teas*
*the shoppin*
*the stories*
*you've kept us safe*
*all those nights Mum's been gone.*

*And I know ya think*
*I'm just the kid with all the swag, yeah*
*the glamour boy.*
*The goals and the glory.*

*The sugar-coated kid with nothin underneath,*
*ridin no-handed down the middle of the street.*

*But right now that's just what I'm doin*
*Ridin no-handed down a street that won't end*
*and y'know I can't find the words like you can bro*

*and I just wanted ya to know.*

And then he's off spirallin
away down the street
shoutin

*Still can't beat me in a sprint though, Natey,*

*can ya dude?*

# Have ya ever felt lost, Sir?

*With no handholds*
*and yer stuck in the tail light of life*
*with it all just spinnin on round ya?*

Mr Joshua's sittin markin maths books
at the end of the day
the last of the masses still ditherin on the playground.

He closes the book,
*Yes, Nate, I have*
*but the thing I want you to understand*
*is that in order to really find yourself*
*you first have to be lost*
*out there in the wilderness.*
*It's nothing to fear*
*and when the darkness comes*
*and you think you can't find a way*
*that's when it happens.*

*Yes, you are lost for now, Nate*
*but only certain people see that darkness*
*and understand*
*that really*
*it's the darkness that switches on the lights.*

*You've got that light, Nate*
*you will re-find who you are*
*and what's happening will change you*
*shape you*
*but that's OK*
*because it will not break you.*

*Dylan will fight, Nate. He will. And you must too.*

He looks out across the playground
to somewhere miles from 'ere.

*In the darkness you will find yourself*
*and your people*
*those who have seen it too*
*those who navigate and find a way.*

*Stick with those people, Nate.*
*Stick with yourself*
*your pen*
*your dreams.*
*Ideas will guide you.*

*You can't ever change*
*things that happen around you*
*all you can do is continue your journey.*

*Whatever happens*
*don't fear the darkness.*

For a few seconds of silence
we're in a dream
clothed in fog

and Mr Joshua's ahead of me
almost out of sight
talkin about darkness
talkin about light

and somewhere I hear feathers movin in the wind.

# Me and Caleb are kickin stones around the playground and talkin about Dylan

when there's a touch on my shoulder
as PS walks past me and bumps fists with Caleb.
He turns to look at me
smiles
kicks a stone over my way.

*Yo, Nate, ya passin it back or what,*
*dude?*

I see Turner watchin us
from the top pitch

fists clenched.

# Me and Jax are allowed to see Dyl

He's lyin on his side
wires   tubes   bleeps
the machine that maps every precious pulse
of his broken heart drawin its crazy patterns.

My spider brother sleeps
strobed in the starlight of a place only he exists.

Mum strokes his hair
whispers, *It's OK.*
Me and Jax are silent
I mean          what is there to say?

# But I remember what I need to say

and lean in and whisper to him
tell him about Caleb's picture of Spiderman
and his wings
tell him it's by his bedside
so he's bein watched over
so he's safe,
tell him I'm waitin for him
out in the wilderness
in the darkness
still clothed in fog,
and I tell him not to be frightened
cos he's not alone in there
I'm with him,
and when I finish
Jax is lookin at me like I'm an alien
but Mum watches    her eyes full of tears.
*That was beautiful, Natey.*

And I see the wilderness in her eyes,
years of it.
A lifetime of things just out of reach
chasin mirages
chasin Jesus,
and I know
I know she's with me in the darkness.

She comes over and hugs me
and we hold hands
and Jax is with us

and we circle and spin.

# That night

I dream about Jesus.

# Back in school

Me and Caleb talk about **Skellig**:
what it means
who he is
what Mina's pictures mean
the wilderness again
the wings, man,
the wings.

# We're sittin eatin Pringles by Dylan's bed

when a doctor comes in
smiles
scratches the ginger stubble on his chin
face that looks like he's not slept since last week
looks over Dylan's little sleepin body
checkin this and checkin that
sits on the end of his bed
clears his throat
taps his fingers on his knee.

*Hello boys*
*I'm one of the doctors here.*
*I know how much of a shock*
*this must have been to you.*
*Has somebody explained what happed to Dylan?*

We nod.

*It's a very rare condition, called endocarditis.*
*I know that's a word*
*you probably won't understand,*
*but basically, Dylan had a problem with his heart*
*that no one knew about when he was born –*
*and this infection's got in*
*and targeted that part of his heart.*

*We've managed to stabilise your brother,*
*but he's going to need to spend quite some time*
*in hospital on a course of antibiotics*
*to try to clear the infection.*

And                    he looks away.

*I'm afraid at this stage there are no guarantees*
*it will clear.*
*If it doesn't, he will need an operation.*

Then quickly –
*But he's in the best place he could possibly be.*
*Talk to him*
*tell him you're here*
*hold his hand.*

He gives Mum a nod.

*I'll leave you alone now for a while.*

# Talk to him Natey

*please darlin*
*my head is empty.*

*We're 'ere, Dyl*
*we're 'ere my brother.*

He looks so beautiful
so peaceful.

*We love ya, Dylan, man,*
*we love ya so much*
*I hope ya can hear me.*

*I hope ya can hear me brother.*

# And then Jax is gone

out onto the ward
runnin
knocks into a trolley and sends stuff flyin
and I'm after him shoutin
but he's so quick
and the corridors are so busy
but I find him
sobbin
curled up in a ball
next to the vendin machines
and I'm sittin on the floor
with his head on my shoulder,
*Jax    brother        we're together.*

# A message to Dylan from across the universe

I'm learnin that sometimes
we hold onto things too long, y'know?
That sometimes we need to learn to let go
and start again.
Leave behind the things we used to want
used to need.

But I'm determined
I will not let go of ya.
And now I need ya to do the same
Dylan
I need ya to hold on as tightly as ya can
and             not             let             go.

Sometimes I'm concrete
like every pore
every cell of my body's solid
and I just can't feel
anythin

but The Beast.

# Y'know what the counsellors would say, right?

They'd say,
*Nate, you've brought yourself up*
*kept it all inside*
*talk about it*
*tell me about yourself*
*your dad*
*your mum*
*your brothers.*

But I'm not doin any of that stuff ever again.
Y'know why?
I can talk with my pen.

# A Question I ask Mr Joshua after school

*How can my head*
*be so full of stuff, Sir*

*so full of sadness*
*so full of questions*
*so full of anger*
*so full of pain*

*yet I am*
*so*
*empty?*

# Michael's baby is poorly

and so is mine.

As Mr Joshua reads
he keeps an eye on me
he knows I know
and when he puts the book down
he sets the class back off workin
and crouches down next to me,

*We can stop reading this you know Nate*
*just let me know.*

*It's fine,          Sir*
*it sorta helps in some weird way y'know?*

*OK Nate*
*OK*
*let me know*
*whatever you need.*

# Texts from PS and Caleb at the same time

I'm here                                          I'm here

# At break, me and Caleb

are just talkin about stuff
tradin          pictures          words          ideas
and PS comes over
fist bumps
he scans Caleb's pictures
watches my words,

*Boys          that's          mint.*

# At night I walk in the rain

past the shops
past school
past the shadows of what used to be.

Through pools of streetlight
lava lanes of traffic
space and time.

An ambulance siren cuts through my mind
as I climb the hill at the back of the park
and sit on the bench
zip my jacket up to the neck.

The city lights glow.

All is not lost, Natey
all is not lost
the words circle above me
high, high above.

I close my eyes and picture Dylan

and send the words across the city on wings of light
past the big coloured pencils
at the Children's Hospital doorway
down the corridors
onto the wards
into his room
above his bed
into his head.

there is light
brother
there is light,
soak it up
brother
turn it into webs and fire 'em back, brother.

# Tonight I dream of you

You know I've been walkin
you know I've been walkin to you all night
and you're propped on your pillow
the early mornin light caught in your hair

and you say to me,
*Natey, why have ya come so far?*
and I say,
*Dylan cos I need ya to know*
*I need ya to know that I came all this way*

*cos I care*
*each step*
*each breath is for you*

and you smile and lay back on your pillow

and as you close your eyes
you whisper to me,
*I love ya*
*big brother*
and now wings of light fold around you
as you sleep
and outside the world is liquid
the world is liquid
but I am flesh and blood
and you are my brother.

# Auntie San's gonna move in for a bit, boys

*I need to be with him*
*y'understand don't ya?*

*Course Mum, no worries.*

I pass her a picture that Caleb's drawn
of Dylan and Spiderman
on the swings in the park together
and make her promise
she'll put it up on the hospital wall
above his bed where she put the other one.

# One night after Jax goes to bed

Auntie San comes and sits with me on the sofa
puts her arm round me,

*Y'know, Natey*     *y'know*     *she does her best*
*yer mum*           *she loves you all so much.*

*She's always been fightin y'know.*

*And I swear*     *all those blokes*
*those*           *muppets*

*since the day I met her*

*I've only ever seen yer dad in her eyes.*

# On the playground

Turner smirks as he passes.
*How's yer little brother Nate?*
*Blow him a kiss from me, will ya?*
Laughs to himself.

# I didn't see where it came from

and neither did Turner
but PS hit him so hard
I heard the air leave Turner's stomach as he fell.

Turner on his feet
swings back
lands flush on PS's cheek
knuckles and kicks
a trail of blood down PS's chin.

Mr Joshua in between 'em
PS is no longer in his body
he's at war
he's an animal at war
blood on his teeth
blood in his words.

# My blood brother is back

And in the darkness we find our people.

# Sorry boys

*chips again, innit,*
says Auntie San,
fag in the side of her mouth
one eye closed.

*Ya want an egg with it?*

To be fair
I don't care.

I'm just glad it's not me doin tea.

# We fall into this weird routine

this half-life
of waitin.

Weeks go by.

Mum at hospital
waitin
us at home
waitin
existin.

Hospital visits
hand holds
head strokes
wings and angels
stories read

Spiderman toys all over the bed
doctors, nurses.

Dyl sleepin sleepin sleepin
fightin fightin fightin

and I examine the spaces between us all
as I try to catch my breath.

I've noticed myself gettin taller everyday
little spots on my forehead
waitin for the man,

waitin for Dylan to beat this thing.

# Early again, Nate? How you doing?

*Come on in for a chat.*
*You want to put the whiteboards out for me?*

When I tell Mr Joshua that Mum messaged
to say Dylan's lookin brighter
and actually laughed about summat last night

he stops dead for a second
and holds my shoulders

and as I hug him
I can feel his hurt
I can feel his joy
I can feel his heavin chest.

# I pass him a poem

All is not lost
in this wilderness world

we sometimes are

sometimes we spiral through black
lost in night
cloaked in dark dreams of cold concrete
and yet
together
the way can be found
one foot
one step
one star
one breath
then another.
All is not lost
all is not lost

I am waiting for you
brother.

## Natey,

he says in a voice from a thousand years ago,
*I missed ya.*
He's the same white as he has been for weeks
and yet in that white
there is light.

We play with his Spiderman figures for a bit
as the nurses busy around us,
askin questions he's got no interest in answerin.

*Just five minutes more please, Nate*
*Dylan needs to rest.*

# As I leave to walk back home

I blow him a kiss
and in return
I get an invisible web fired at me.

*See ya later*
*Turbo Terror,*
*Mum'll be 'ere in a bit.*

# In the doctor's side room,

well, the paediatric cardiologist
if ya wanna be clever,
he's doin the finger-tappin thing again.

*As you know*
*Dylan is making progress*
*but we are aware the infection is still there.*
*For now,*
*all the doctors think*
*the best course of action*
*is to continue the antibiotics*
*and hope that it clears.*

He glances out the window
as the city streets take on the sheen of rain.

Smiles a smile that really in't a smile at all.

# Message from PS

Nate I'm so sorry, man, can we talk?

# He passes me a KitKat

and as I slide my nail down the silver foil
to snap it in half
he talks,

*I'm so sorry*
*Nate*
*I*
*I*
*I just*
*dunno,*
*I dunno what happened*
*I just...*

*PS,*
*man,*
*forget it,*
*you're 'ere*
*I'm 'ere.*
*Now shuddup goin on*
*and fire up the Xbox, dude,*
*there's a can of whoopass*
*about to be opened all over ya.*

Knuckles touch
the space between us gone
the river runs.

# Dylan gets stronger every day

The doctors say he's doin well,
but when they talk about the future
they always hesitate

as if they're holdin summat back.

# We kick into SATs overdrive

Past papers comin out our ears
readin between the lines
stupid reasonin questions I'll never need
infinitives and rubbish like that.

Even the readin papers are stupid
I mean
some muppet claimin to know
what a poem's about,
givin it a right and wrong answer,
man, some people are stupid.

Mr Joshua's good at keepin the chill on things,
*Just hoops to jump through, guys,*
*that's all they are*
*try your best*
*you know what I think of you all.*

*Soon it'll all be over*
*and it's freewheeling all the way to high school,*
*transition days*
*new uniforms*
*stepping stones to a new life.*

*And what do I always say guys…*
and then the song's on again.
*Every little thing…*

# We finish Skellig

but we keep talkin about it –
chalk drawins on black paper
drama
the display board fills up with
wings
owls
angels.

The idea, man,
of summat
watchin over the baby
keepin it safe
wings
light.

Angels in the hospital,
angels in the classroom.

## Me and PS and Caleb are sittin in the dinin hall

and Mr Joshua comes in
to get a dinner from the cook
watches us eat
and I just know what he's gonna say
before he even says it,

*Three little birds.*

# The phone call

comes in the middle of the night
the week before SATs start.

Auntie San's mobile vibrates on the kitchen table
where she sits face down,
3 empty cider cans and a half-finished pack of fags.

As I get off the sofa bed
I know it'll be Mum.

And summat's happened

to Dylan.

# Auntie San orders an Uber

and I wake Jax.
*Dude, Mum says we need to go hospital.*
Jax pulls his joggers on
He whispers, *What's wrong, Nate?*
*I dunno Jax*
*I dunno.*

And when he hugs me
he's cryin.
And we breathe together.

# The hospital's dead

But Dylan's room's alive with doctors
and when Mum comes out to see us
I see that she's steppin out of herself.
*It's happened again*, she says,
her ghost-mouth formin words
she dun't wanna say.

And in the darkness of the Family Room
we wait.

We wait until Mum tells us we need to go home with Auntie San and get some sleep

Sleep?                                    What's that, man?

# Caleb and PS listen to me at break

They're tellin' me to breathe

but The Beast is risin.

# Mr Joshua says

BIDMAS stands for

**B**rackets
**I**ndices
**D**ivision
**M**ultiplication
**A**ddition
**S**ubtraction

# The Beast says

BIDMAS stands for

Brother
Is
Dyin
Make
A
Scene

# The concrete cracks and crumbles

and falls apart and I'm aware that The Beast
is about to be released and this time I don't care
I don't care about breathin techniques or self-regulation
blood rushes to my head and swirls behind my eyeballs
fire and smoke      smoke and fire
I knock the pen pot over      shatterin the steel silence
of the maths lesson

I catch Caleb's kind eyes      but I'm gone, man,
I push back my chair      and the table's turned

Mr Joshua is a blur somewhere far far away
from where I am right now      walkin through fire
he empties the kids from the classroom
as each pen pot and table's upturned      chairs kicked
I've no idea   what I'm doin      but whatever it is
I just need to feel      to feel summat
I'm shoutin      I'm shoutin
words that come from some other place
and when it's done  I collapse into a ball
screwed up like a rubbish poem
chairs and tables and pens all around me
lost in a destruction zone of my own makin.

Mr Joshua's standin by the whiteboard
breathin hard        he steps towards me and
gently helps me to my feet,

*Nate, it's OK        it's OK,*

and I wanna tell him it's not OK
everything's not gonna be alright
but I'm a concrete block     a castle again
and I'm tired         I'm tired      and cold
and he swallows me up in his arms
and holds me,

*I'm here, Nate*

*I'm here.*

# Auntie San takes a big drag of her fag

*Natey*          *Jax*

.

*they've got him back again.*

# She blows a smoke ring

*We need to get down to hospital*
*and find out what happens now.*
*Eat ya chips, boys.*
*We all need our strength.*

As Jax pours a ridiculous amount
of vinegar over his food,
San winks at me:
*I've spoken to Mr Joshua and Mrs Jones*
*about what happened today, Nate.*
*They're fine.*
*It's sorted.*
*They know how much pressure*
*you're under with Dylan*
*and all them tests next week.*
*They know ya can do it, kid.*
*Let's not worry ya mum with this, eh?*

She winks and smiles.

*Fighters aren't we, eh?*

*C'mon boys, let's go see Dyl.*

# The little machine

maps a beatin heart again
keep drawin yer lines little machine
keep drawin yer lines.

Dylan smiles: *Hey, Natey. Hey, Jax.*


We sit on the edge of his bed
while Mum talks to the white coats.

Three little birds.

When the docs go,
Mum talks about the operation,
*It needs to be quick boys cos Dyl's heart is weak...*
*so weak...*
*and*
*Jesus...*
*I need a drink boys...*

Jax goes over and gives Mum a hug.

*They wanna operate next week, Natey,*
*on Monday*
*but I know you've got ya tests to do –*
*ya want me to send Auntie San in to sort it?*

*Nah Mum, it's fine*
*one foot in front of the other, innit?*

*Hey, Natey.*

*Yes, Turbo Terror?*

*I'm SPIDEYMAN!*

*Yes you are*
*brother.*
*Yes you are.*

# I miss the grammar, punctuation and spellin test on Monday

stay in bed
watchin my phone.

Auntie San goes into school first thing:
*they say to go back in Wednesday, Natey*
*they say ya can catch up.*

Me on the sofa
Jax upstairs
San in the kitchen

  I

watch

the

minutes

roll

over

on

my

phone

I listen to the pulse of my heart
and try not to think

about scalpels.

# San's phone rings

I bury my head under my duvet.

When it's torn off me,
San and Jax
are wide-eyed.

# Natey, it's done

*it's done, Natey.*

# Tuesday is sunlight

and me and Jax and Auntie San
on the bus with pasties
singin stoopid songs.


As we pass the park
I notice how beautiful the blossom trees are
and how I normally notice 'em
as soon as the buds start to form


and I've missed so much
but now I notice.


And I can smile.

# Auntie San dusts pastry flakes off her jeans

*Y'know boys*
*y'know, how much I love you all?*

Jax is on his phone, listenin with one ear.

*Auntie San,* I ask,
*did ya never want kids?*

And she's still dustin pastry off her jeans

even though it's all gone.

She coughs,

looks above my head into the distance
out at the city
and I think she might cry.

Flashes a gold tooth
kisses my cheek,

*Nah, Natey*
*I've got you lot*

*what more could I need?*

# Dylan's asleep

his little chest covered in wires
and a big white gauze thing

but the machine is movin

and Mum and the doctors
have a new light in their eyes


and he's watched over by angels.

# So when I go in on Wednesday

I do the arithmetic and the reasonin paper
with the rest of the class,
but I'm not allowed to go and play out
or speak to PS and Caleb
until I've done the papers I missed,
just in case they've memorised the entire test
and tell me every single question and answer.

*It's a stupid rule, I know, Nate*
*and I'm sorry*
*you know I don't agree with this sort of thing*
*but we have to follow them.*

*And Nate*
*I spoke to your mum*
*I can't tell you how pleased I am*
*that Dylan's operation went well.*

And when I look up at Mr Joshua
our eyes are full.

# We go see Dyl at the weekend

And the gauze thing on his chest has gone.
And he's sittin up on his bed
dead proud of the big run of staples
all the way up his chest.

*Look Natey, look:*

*it's a ladder, Natey*

*a ladder to the stars.*

And I grab his hand.
His beautiful hot little hand.
And kiss it
and kiss it
and kiss it.

# Back to the blur of hospital visits

and Auntie San's 'cookin'.

Watchin Dyl get out of bed
and start walkin again,
make that start runnin again.
The nurses and doctors can't believe how a kid
that's been through what he's been through
can have so much energy.

Mum's changin
like someone's pumped her back up again
like a balloon.

She talks about plans for Dylan to come home
how life can re-start again

how she can get back to Bingo.

# I watch a pair of swifts rollercoastin the skies above the hospital

I'd always feel sorry for 'em, man,
comin all the way through the dark
and the weather
all those miles out at sea
to spend summer flyin above this city
but now I salute 'em.

My arms are wings
and I'm with 'em.
*Welcome back,* I shout,
*welcome home.*

# Me and Caleb and PS

walk towards the high school
we'll be at in September
and talk about what today's transition stuff's
gonna be like.

Just then,
Turner comes past on a mountain bike.
*Out the way, muppets,* he shouts,
*yer gonna get eaten alive!*

We three shake our heads
together.

# Turner's nowhere to be seen when we get there

but we hear it straight away
from the cracklin corridor gossip

the bike he was on was stolen.

One of his thick-headed brothers
probably grabbed it off some poor kid
and Turner's just jumped on it

but that poor kid is in Year 9
and spotted Turner on it
as soon as he got to school.


Turner's transition is spent in isolation.

# We laugh through the daft little badges we make

we laugh as we wander down the corridors
we laugh through maths
and we laugh through PE
and the walk home.

# As we pass Poppy Field

we see Mr Joshua in the classroom singin to himself

he catches sight of us and waves out the window,

*See you tomorrow boys,*
*you know what we say, hey?*
*Come on now boys, tell me how it is!*

*Every little thing gonna be alright, Sir!*

He gives us a thumbs up,
salutes us
and goes back to his singin.

# Jax is out on the street

with a couple of his mates
kickin a ball around,
*How was it Nate, ya got a girlfriend yet?*

*Leave it out Jax, give a man a bit of time*
*just been puttin the vibe out, innit.*

*Oh Nate,*
*Mum's home.*

# I can hear 'em laughin before I'm even through the front door

I drop my bag and find 'em at the kitchen table
two cans deep
heads back
roarin.

*Hey Natey! Yer home!*

The house smells of cider
and bleach
and fags
and cheap perfume
and I get onto my little sofa bed
and soak up
every
last
bit
of it.

# As I'm rinsin out the last of the cardboard coco þoþs from my bowl

Mum comes in and lights a fag,
*The doctors say Dylan should be home soon.*
*They've kept him in much longer*
*than they normally would*
*cos they wanted to be sure, to be really sure*
*that everythin was workin*
*and that the infection*
*wasn't just gonna leap straight back in there,*
*y'know?*

*They reckon his heart*
*should be better than it ever was.*
*Jesus, what a kid eh?*
*Nate*
*I'm so sorry I've been gone for so long.*
*It feels like I've been gone forever, y'know?*

*I'm so proud of ya, love.*

*Mum*
*yer 'ere now*
*that's all that matters.*

# On the last day of school

we do all the stuff we've been waitin for
the parties
the assembly
the old guy handin things out
the shirt signins
the singin

and in the afternoon sun
as we play the most disorganised
sweat-drenched game of rounders
you've ever seen in yer life,
Mr Joshua comes over to me.

*How you doing, Nate?*

*Alright, Sir, I'm alright*
*I really am.*

He smiles and takes his shades off.

*Told you it would be didn't I, eh?*

*Now listen, Nate,*
*do you remember way back at the start of the year*
*when I told you I was proud of you*
*even though I didn't know you?*

*Well, Nate, I am so proud to know you now.*
*So, so proud.*

*I want you to know*
*that even when you're at high school*
*I'll still be here, OK?*

*Any time you want to drop in and say hi,*
*that'd be cool –*
*and don't forget me when you're a famous poet, eh?*
*I want a whole book dedicated to me, OK?*

*Sure, Sir, no problem*
*and Sir –*
*thank you, Sir.*

We bump fists.

*In the darkness we find our people, eh, Nate?*

*Yes, Sir, I guess we do.*

# He runs back to the classroom

and I see him openin his desk drawer.
As he walks back over
he's grinnin and hidin summat behind his back.

Gets me to close my eyes.

When I open 'em

he's holdin out his copy of **Skellig**.

*Nate*
*take this*

*it's yours.*

# He's written inside:

*Never forget to do what you must.*

# The final five minutes of the final year

take forever to pass, man.

Outside, the playground heaves
with sunburnt parents
a few beers down already
by the look of most of 'em.

When the classroom door finally opens
we flow out huggin and cheerin and dancin.

Me and PS and Caleb are high-fivin
and back-slappin and laughin
and Turner's off out the gates on his own,

gone till September.

# As we wade through the stream

of parents and kids and prams
I turn back to the classroom
and see Mr Joshua watchin us.

He raises a hand and salutes me
and he's noddin
and he laughs.

I salute back
wave
and I can't hear him, but I know what he's sayin,


*EVERY LITTLE THING GONNA BE ALRIGHT!*

# PART 6
# THE FINAL POEM

We walk across the last few metres
of the playground
for the last time
together
me and PS and Caleb.

*Can't believe it,* PS says.
*Can't believe we're 'ere for the last time.*

Caleb goes: *I know, man, crazy, innit?*
*Good times!*   I shout.   *Good times!*

PS gives me a little push on the shoulder,
starts runnin ahead of me,
Shouts, *For sure!*
*Many more to come though, eh, Nate?*
*Let's go, man, let's go!*

And I'm by his side        Caleb catches up
out through the gates
into the big wide world
into summat strange and new.

And there's Jax and Auntie San
waitin outside the corner shop with freeze pops
smilin.

Then          I                    hear          him,

*NAAAAATTTTTEEEEEEYYYYY
I'M FLYYYYYYYING!
I can touch the
SKYYYYYYYYYYYYYYYYYYYYYYYYYYY!!!!!!!!!!!!
I'm SPIIIIIIIIIIIIIIIIDDDDDEEEEYYYYYYYYY
MAAAAAAAAAAAAN!
NAAAAATTTTTEEEEEEYYYYY!*

High as a kite on the swings in the park,
Mum wavin from the bench
and he sees me          God knows how but he does.


As we reach 'em          Mum's on her feet
and we're gone          both of us          all of us
and now Dylan's 'ere and he's hot and sweaty
and loud and
Dylan's 'ere, man, Dylan's 'ere.

*Chinese tonight to celebrate, eh, Natey?* Mum says.
*Have whatever ya want,
we'll live on toast for a week if we have to.
We've got so much to celebrate.*

*All I want is number 27 and 53, Mum.
Food of the gods.*

She looks at me all confused
but still smilin anyway.

And she's just about to speak
when I think I hear someone shout my name
from far away across the park

and I look over

and there's a silhouette
of a man
and he's shoutin my name

and he's walkin towards us

and I stare

and I swear
as he steps outta the sun
the man looks



like


Jesus.

# Acknowledgements

First of all, I'd like to say an enormous thank you to Dr Edmund J Ladusans, Consultant Paediatric Cardiologist at Manchester Children's Hospital for his generosity of time and knowledge in reading this book and helping us to understand and articulate Dylan's condition authentically. He treated Dylan as if he was a real-life flesh and blood patient, and for his kindness and care I'm eternally grateful. Long live the NHS.

The Rainbow Trust Children's Charity supports families, like Nate's, who have a child with a life-threatening or terminal illness: https://www.rainbowtrust.org.uk/

Secondly, to David Almond, who alongside Alan Garner is, in my opinion, the greatest living writer for children and young people in the English language. David's books taught me about the importance of place and voice and spirit. You're a genius.

Thanks also to Joe Todd-Stanton for his thoughtful and poignant illustrations, which elevate the words, take us directly into Nate's world and create deeper connections between the text and the readers.

Finally, thanks to my editor, the incredible Charlotte Hacking for her patience, care and efficiency at forcing me to tell this story better. From the first time she saw this book, when it was barely more than a tenuous set of threads tangled across pages of random poems, she believed in it – and my ability to craft its message. I couldn't have done it without you.

# ABOUT THE POET AND THE ILLUSTRATOR

## MATT GOODFELLOW

Former primary school teacher Matt Goodfellow is now a prize-winning poet who visits schools across the UK to give hugely popular, high-energy performances and workshops. His first poetry collection for Otter-Barry Books, *Chicken on the Roof*, received wide acclaim. He is also the author of *Caterpillar Cake*, illustrated by Krina Patel-Sage and shortlisted for the CLiPPA award in 2022, *Shu-Lin's Grandpa*, illustrated by Yu Rong and shortlisted for the CILIP Kate Greenaway Medal 2022, and a contributor to CLiPPA-shortlisted poetry collection *Being Me: Poems about Thoughts, Worries and Feelings*, all published by Otter-Barry Books. His latest poetry collection, *Let's Chase Stars Together*, was shortlisted for the CLiPPA award 2023. Matt lives in Stockport.

## JOE TODD-STANTON

grew up in Brighton and has a first class degree in Illustration from UWE, Bristol. He is a widely acclaimed author and illustrator of picture books and graphic novels.
*The Secret of Black Rock* was longlisted for the CILIP Kate Greenaway Award and won the Waterstones Children's Book Prize. *The Comet* won the Shadowers' Choice Award for the Yoto Carnegie Medal for Illustration, 2023. Joe lives in London.